ALI BABA
AND THE FORTY THIEVES

STONE ARCH BOOKS
a capstone imprint

ALI BABA
AND THE FORTY THIEVES

RETOLD BY MATTHEW K. MANNING
ILLUSTRATED BY RICARDO OSNAYA

DESIGNER: BRANN GARVEY   ART DIRECTOR: BOB LENTZ

EDITOR: DONALD LEMKE   CREATIVE DIRECTOR: HEATHER KINDSETH

ASSOC. EDITOR: SEAN TULIEN   EDITORIAL DIRECTOR: MICHAEL DAHL

Published by Stone Arch Books, A Capstone Imprint 151 Good Counsel Drive, P.O. Box 669 Mankato, Minnesota 56002 www.capstonepub.com Copyright © 2011 by Stone Arch Books All rights reserved. No part of this publication may be reproduced in whole or in part, or stored in a retrieval system, or transmitted in any form or by any means, electronic, mechanical, photocopying, recording, or otherwise, without written permission of the publisher.

Cataloging-in-Publication Data is available on the Library of Congress website.

ISBN: 978-1-4342-1988-6 (library binding)
ISBN: 978-1-4342-2776-8 (paperback)

Summary: The story of Ali Baba, a young Persian boy who discovers a cave filled with gold and jewels, the hidden treasures of forty deadly thieves. Unfortunately, his greedy brother, Kasim, cannot wait to get his hands on the riches. Returning to the cave, he is captured by the thieves and killed, and now the evil men want revenge on Ali Baba as well.

Printed in the United States of America in Stevens Point, Wisconsin.
032010
005741WZF10

CONTENTS

CAST OF CHARACTERS

KASIM

ALI BABA

ALI BABA'S WIFE

MARJANA

ALI BABA'S SON

THE CAPTAIN ...
AND HIS 39 THIEVES

All right, men, let's move!

The day's not done yet!!

You heard the captain, boys.

Stash the treasure in the cave.

Several hours later . . .

KRRRRRR

ZZZZZZZ

Huh —? What was that?

The next morning . . .

KNOCK!

KNOCK!

KNOCK!

So how much gold is left in the cave?!

Sigh! Come in, Kasim.

My wife told you?

Surely you'll share your findings, Ali Baba?

Don't you have enough money already?

Haven't I taught you anything, little brother . . . ?

Meanwhile, at the cavern . . .

Good ride, men.

Let's see how our visitor is keeping, shall we?

OPEN SESAME!!

Where is he?!

I thought I told you to stake his body to the wall!

We did, Captain!

Then it appears we've had another intruder . . .

. . . and he didn't take our little warning to heart.

Unload your treasures, men! We're headed to the city.

Someone there must know what happened to the body.

After all, the funeral couldn't have been very pleasant.

Excuse me. Have you witnessed any funerals in the city lately?

No.

How about you, boy. Seen anything unusual?

No, sir.

I don't know what you're talking about.

This is useless —

Wait! Listen . . .

I'm telling you, friend, this was the strangest job I've ever had . . .

I'm glad you're all moving in here.

I was getting lonely without Kasim.

Yes, I think it's for the best.

Is that everything, Marjana?

Yes, Ali Baba. Thank you.

I just hope Father feels the same.

Moments later . . .

You sure we haven't met before? You look familiar.

No, I think I would remember.

But that reminds me. Perhaps I should check on my horses, if you don't mind —

Gentlemen! If I may have your attention!

Just beautiful, wasn't she?

Rumor has it she saved his life.

I can't believe she used to be a servant girl.

So happy we could make it, my dear.

What was that song they played earlier?

Excuse me for a minute, sweetheart.

There you are, Father. We were looking for you.

And I, you. I wanted to give you my wedding gift.

Your stubborn mule?

62

ARABIAN NIGHTS

The story of "Ali Baba and the Forty Thieves" is part of a collection of Middle Eastern and South Asian folktales known as *One Thousand and One Nights.* These tales have been passed down from generation to generation for hundreds of years. The first English-language edition, titled *The Arabian Nights' Entertainment,* was published in 1706.

Since then, many versions of the book have been published — some containing more than 1,000 stories. In each of these editions, the tales of mystery and adventure are told by the same narrator, a beautiful woman named Scheherazade. She has just married an evil ruler who plans to kill her before the night is through. To stop him, Scheherazade entertains the king with a new story each night, and he soon forgets about his deadly plan.

The Arabian Nights tales remain some of the greatest stories ever told. They include popular adventures, such as "The Fisherman and the Genie," "The Seven Voyages of Sinbad," and "Ali Baba and the Forty Thieves." Many of these stories have been adapted into movies, books, and plays that are still popular today.

HIDDEN TREASURES

In 1520, Spanish explorer Hernando Cortes and his men raided the Aztec empire, stealing the treasure of their emperor, Montezuma. Before the Spanish crew could escape, the Aztecs attacked, and the jewels were spilled and buried around Lake Tezcuco, near modern day Mexico City. Despite many efforts, these treasures have never been found.

Edward Thatch, the pirate known as Blackbeard, plundered the high seas in the early 1700s, stealing gold and other riches. He died in 1718, but his treasure was never found. Many still believe it's hidden somewhere in the Caribbean Sea.

In 1922, archeologist Howard Carter found the tomb of Egyptian pharaoh Tutankhamen, also know as King Tut, which was filled with millions of dollars in gold and jewels. However, many believe other tombs remain hidden, waiting to be discovered.

ABOUT THE AUTHOR

Matthew K. Manning is a comic book writer, historian, and fan. Over the course of his career, he's written comics or books starring Batman, Superman, Iron Man, Wolverine, Spider-Man, the Incredible Hulk, the Legion of Super-Heroes, the Justice League, and even Bugs Bunny. Some of his more recent works include DK Publishing's *Marvel Chronicle* and Running Press's *The Batman Vault*. He is currently writing a mini-series for the DC Comics imprint Wildstorm. He lives in Brooklyn, New York, with his wife Dorothy and a baby girl on the way.

ABOUT THE ILLUSTRATOR

Ricardo Osnaya is a self-taught illustrator, living and working in Mexico. Since first publishing editorial illustrations in *Excelsior Magazine*, Osnaya has made a name for himself as a freelance artist. He's published the comics *Burundis* and *Dos Guerreros* and illustrated popular characters, such as the Power Rangers. Currently, Osnaya collaborates with Protobunker Studio and works as a comic and illustration instructor at the Mexican Institute of Youth and other schools.

GLOSSARY

arrangement *(uh-RAYNJ-muhnt)*—plans for something to happen, such as a funeral service

basin *(BAY-suhn)*—a large bowl used for washing

caravan *(KA-ruh-van)*—a group of people or vehicles traveling together

cargo *(KAR-goh)*—freight that is carried by some form of transportation, such as a mule

cavern *(KAV-ern)*—a large cave

courtyard *(KORT-yard)*—an open area surrounded by walls

curiosity *(kyur-ee-AHSS-i-tee)*—an eagerness to find out

gruesome *(GROO-suhm)*—disgusting or horrible

inform *(in-FORM)*—to tell someone something

intruder *(in-TROOD-uhr)*—a person who forces their way into a place where they are not wanted

secure *(si-KYOOR)*—safe, firmly closed, or well protected

sesame *(SESS-uh-mee)*—a small oval seed, which comes from a tropical plant

stubborn *(STUHB-urn)*—hard to deal with

tailor *(TAY-lur)*—someone who makes or alters clothes

DISCUSSION QUESTIONS

1. Ali Baba stole from the thieves because he needed money for his family. Do you think stealing is ever right? Explain your answer.

2. Marjana kills the evil captain. She believes this action is the only way to protect herself and her family. Do you think her decision was okay? Why or why not?

3. At the end of the story, Ali Baba tells his son the secret password to the treasure cave. Do you think Ali Baba's son will use the password to get more riches? Explain.

WRITING PROMPTS

1. Write a final chapter to this book. What happens next? Does Ali Baba's son go back to the cave? Do the authorities ever find out about the missing thieves? You decide.

2. If you had a cave full of treasure, what would you buy? Write a story describing how you would use the riches.

3. Imagine your own Arabian Nights tale. Think of a story filled with mystery and adventure. Then write it down and read it to friends and family.

STONE ARCH BOOKS

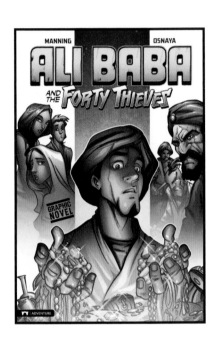

ALADDIN AND THE MAGIC LAMP

The legendary tale of Aladdin, a poor youth living in the city of Al Kal'as. One day, the crafty boy outsmarts an evil sorcerer, getting his hands on a magical lamp that houses a wish-fulfilling genie! Soon, all of Aladdin's dreams come true, and he finds himself married to a beautiful princess. All is well until, one day, the evil sorcerer returns to reclaim the lamp.

ALI BABA AND THE FORTY THIEVES

The legendary tale of Ali Baba, a young Persian boy who discovers a cave filled with gold and jewels, the hidden treasures of forty deadly thieves. Unfortunately, his greedy brother, Kasim, cannot wait to get his hands on the riches. Returning to the cave, he is captured by the thieves and killed, and now the evil men want revenge on Ali Baba as well.

ARABIAN NIGHTS TALES

THE SEVEN VOYAGES OF SINBAD

The tale of Sinbad the Sailor, who goes to sea in search of great riches and discovers even greater adventures. On his seven treacherous voyages, the Persian explorer braves a shipwreck, fights off savage cannibals, and battles a giant Cyclops, hoping to survive and tell his legendary story.

THE FISHERMAN AND THE GENIE

The legendary tale of an evil Persian king, who marries a new wife each day and then kills her the next morning. To stop this murderous ruler, a brave woman named Scheherazade risks her own life and marries the king herself . . . but not without a plan. On their wedding night, she will entertain him with the tale of the Fisherman and the Genie — a story so amazing, he'll never want it to end.